D0116895

Five Little Kittens

by Nancy Jewell

pictures by Elizabeth Sayles

Clarion Books • New York

Clarion Books
a Houghton Mifflin Company imprint
215 Park Avenue South, New York, NY 10003
Text copyright © 1999 by Nancy Jewell
Illustrations copyright © 1999 by Elizabeth Sayles

The illustrations for this book were executed in pastel.
The text was set in 34/42-point Gararond-Light.

Printed in Singapore.

Library of Congress Cataloging-in-Publication Data

Jewell, Nancy.
Five little kittens / by Nancy Jewell ; illustrated by Eizabeth Sayles.
p.   cm.
Summary: Five little kittens get bathed with Mama's tongue, enjoy
breakfast, play and do their chores, have fish soup at lunchtime, and go to bed.
ISBN 0-395-77517-5
[1. Cats—Fiction. 2. Day—Fiction. 3. Stories in rhyme.]
I. Sayles, Elizabeth, ill. II. Title.
Pz8.3.J47Fi   1999
[E]—dc21   98-31226
CIP
AC

TWP   10   9   8   7   6   5   4   3   2   1

For Brittney
—N.J.
For Jessica and Matthew
—E.S.

Five little kittens
lived in a house
with their mama and papa
and their little toy mouse.

Every morning
promptly at nine,
the five little kittens
stood in a line.

Then Mama Cat bathed them
one by one,
licking each kitten
with her rough, pink tongue.

For breakfast she gave them
cream in a dish
with a little hot porridge
and a bite of fish.

The kittens fed
their little toy mouse
a bowl of toy porridge
in his little toy house.

Then Papa Cat wiped
his bowl and dish,
and gave the five kittens
each a kiss.

"I'm off to work,"
Papa Cat said.
"Be good little kittens,
and make your bed."

16

The kittens played tag
and did their chores,
and when they were done
they played some more.

Papa got home
on the dot of noon,
and served fish soup
with a big wooden spoon.

The kittens fed
their little toy mouse
a toy fish bun
in his little toy house.

Then the kittens curled up
in their mama's lap,
and while she brushed them
they took a long nap.

At the tail end of day
when supper was done,
Mama bathed those kittens
one by one.

The kittens said good night
to their little toy mouse,
and tucked him into bed
in his little toy house.

Then Mama and Papa
told the kittens good night,
gave them five kisses,
and turned out the light.

The End